HANG GLIDING & PARAGLIDING

John Allan

www.hungrytomato.com

First published in 2022 by Hungry Tomato Ltd.

F1, Old Bakery Studios,
Blewetts Wharf, Malpas Road,
Truro, Cornwall, TR1 1QH, UK

A CIP catalogue record for this book is available from the British Library.

Manufactured in the USA.

ISBN 978 1 914087 18 9

Picture credits
(t=top; b=bottom; c=center; l=left; r=right)

Age Fotostock/Superstock: 42t. Denis Balibouse: 38/39t, 44. Denis Balibouse/Red Bull Photofiles: 38b. Bettmann/Corbis: 8/9t. Elizabeth Czitronyi/Alamy: 43t. Steve Elkins: 15b. Flybubble Paragliding School, www.flybubble.co.uk: 23t. Getty Images: 7t, 7b. Ulrich Grill/Red Bull Photofiles: 25tr. John Heiney: 45b. INSADCO Photography/Alamy: 34t. Vitek Ludvik/Red Bull Photofiles: 22. Alfredo Martinez/Red Bull Photofiles: 16/17t. Mary Evans Picture Library: 5c. Ian Mills, 10fifty.com: 15tr. Paraglidingshop.co.uk: 27t. Christian Pondella/Red Bull Photofiles: 39b. Francois Portmann/Red Bull Photofiles: 41c. The Print Collector/Alamy: 6. Bill Ross/Corbis: 23b. Pasi Salminen/Red Bull Photofiles: 41tr. Shutterstock: 1, 2, 3, 10t, 11cl, 12, 13t, 13b, 16c, 18, 19bl x 3, 21 all, 26, 33b, 35tr, 46/47. Bernhard Spöttel/Red Bull Photofiles: 36. Square1.com: 27br. Noel Whittall: 8b, 9b, 14/15t, 20, 29b, 31t, 31b, 32/33t, 32b, 35bl, 37t, 37b, 40t, 43t, 45t. Wikipedia: 28/29t, 30. Wingsofrogallo.org: 19tr. David Wootton: 4/5t, 13c, 24tt, 27c, 52cr. Tim Wright/Corbis: 28b.

Every effort has been made to trace copyright holders, and we apologize in advance for any omissions. We would be pleased to insert the appropriate acknowledgements in any subsequent edition of this publication.

Neither the publishers nor the author shall be liable for any bodily harm or damage to property whatsoever that may be caused or sustained as a result of conducting any of the activities featured in this book.

CONTENTS

FIRST FLIGHTS

THE BASICS

THE GEAR

GLIDERS

COMPETITION

PEOPLE AND PLACES

OVERVIEW

Nearly 1,500 years ago in China, people first tried flying. Many people were hurt or killed trying to fly.

Then, in the 1900s, people who wanted to fly began studying birds. They realized that gliding birds do not need to flap their wings to fly.

People began hang gliding in the 1960s. Paragliders followed in the 1980s.

Hang gliders have stiff wings. Paragliders are soft, like parachutes.

An early attempt at flying

EARLY HISTORY

Otto Lilienthal in a test flight

Otto Lilienthal, Germany

The first great hang glider was Otto Lilienthal.

He made wings out of wood and canvas in the 1880s. He hung from his glider by his armpits.

Chanute's assistant, Augustus Moore Herring, flying the biplane glider

Octave Chanute, USA

In 1896, Octave Chanute built a biplane glider. His assistant tested the glider on sand dunes by Lake Michigan, USA. A biplane has two wings.

THE FIRST GLIDERS

The Wright brothers built and flew the first aircraft in 1903. This flight took place in Kitty Hawk, North Carolina, USA.

An early Rogallo glider

In the 1950s, Dr Francis Rogallo invented parachutes for spacecraft. His ideas were used to create hang gliders. These were called 'Rogallos'. The modern hang glider was invented in 1963 by Australian, John Dickenson.

Wilbur Wright watches Orville Wright

An early ram-air parachute

The paraglider

In 1978, a group of Frenchmen began jumping off mountains in a new type of parachute. They called it the ram-air parachute.

Companies began making these parachutes and named them paragliders.

HOW GLIDERS FLY

Gliders do not need a motor, they use the rising air to fly. Rising air is called lift.

The large wing of a glider keeps its front (leading) edge tilted up higher than its back (trailing) edge as it flies. This means air is pushed downwards. The wing reacts to this by trying to rise.

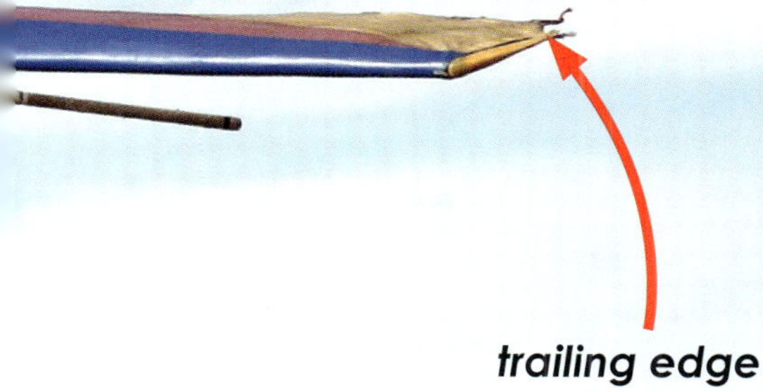

There are three types of natural lift:

Ridge lift When wind meets a hill, it is forced upwards. This ridge lift helps pilots to climb higher.

Thermal lift Thermals are patches of air that have been made extra warm by the sun. Thermals can take gliders up very high.

Wave lift This happens when wind flows down the back of one hill and is 'bounced' up when it meets the front of the next hill. Wave lift is smooth and powerful.

Staying up

A glider needs to push downhill all the time to stay up. This is like riding a bike without pedals!

CONTROLLING A GLIDER

All aircraft use three types of movement: roll, pitch and yaw. Hang glider pilots swing their bodies to keep control.

Roll

Roll means tilting one wing lower than the other. The pilot tilts the wing by shifting their body sideways. This causes the glider to turn.

Pitch

Pitch means tilting the front of the glider up or down. This controls the speed. Pulling forwards speeds the glider up. Pushing back slows it down.

Yaw

Yaw is when one side of the glider is moved forwards, causing the glider to turn. When the right-hand side of the glider is moved forwards, the glider moves to the left.

THE HANG GLIDER

This is the basic set-up of a hang glider.

The **wing** material fits over the main frame. It is called the sail. Several ribs, called **battens**, are sewn into each side.

The **hang point** is a strong loop on the **keel** at the center of the **control frame.**

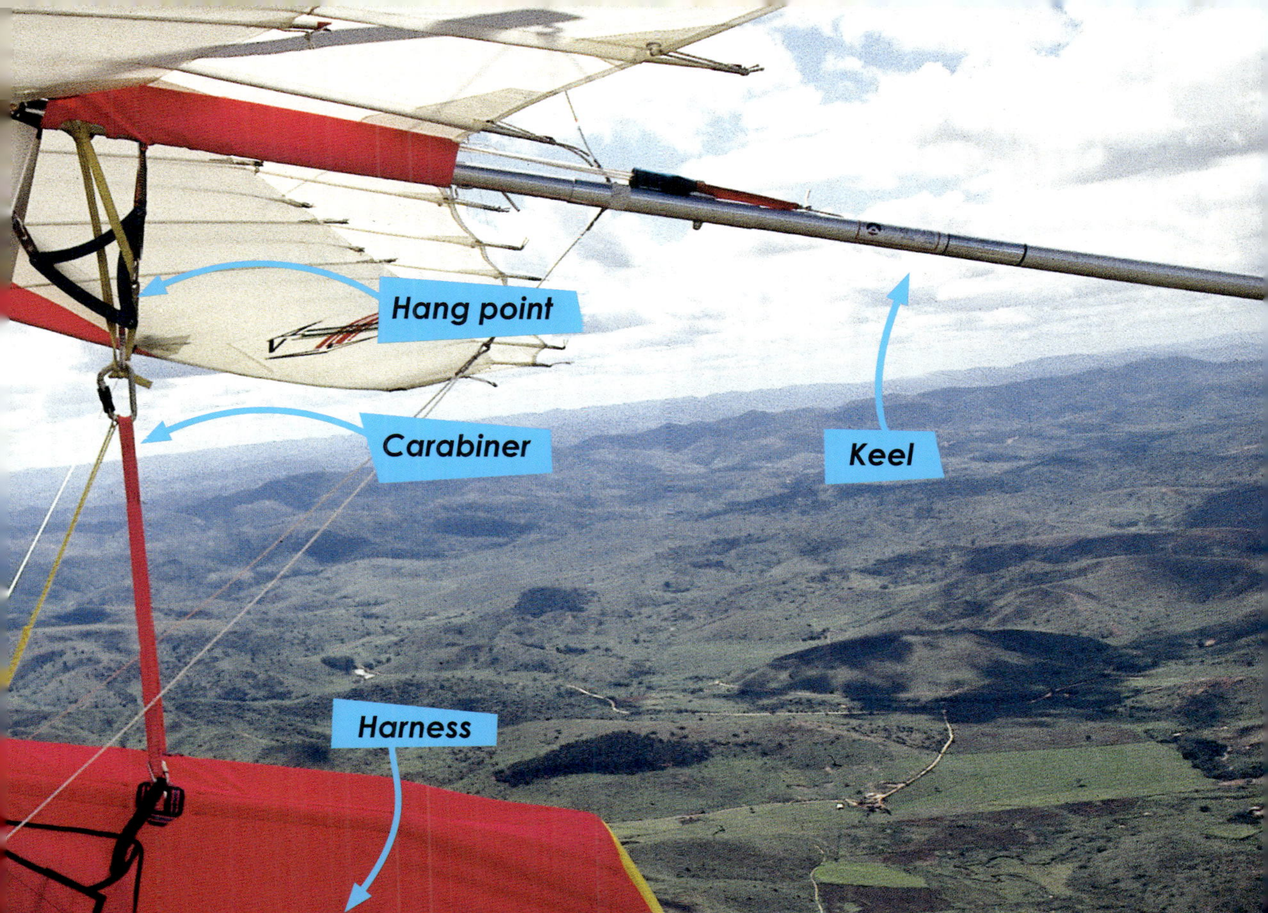

Quick-release catches make the glider easy to put together for flight

The **harness** joins to the hang point with a **carabiner.** The carabiner carries the pilot's weight.

THE PARAGLIDER

Paraglider wings are inflated with air. This is called the ram-air effect. The wings are called canopies.

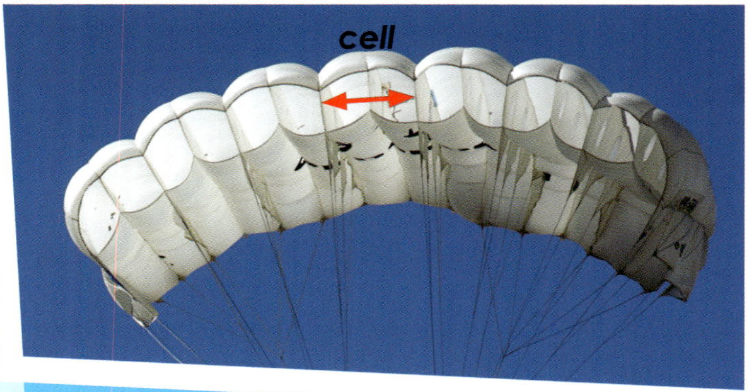

The **canopy** is built from many cells that are sewn together side by side. Each cell is open at the front and closed at the back.

The pilot sits in a **harness** that is attached to the canopy by many lines.

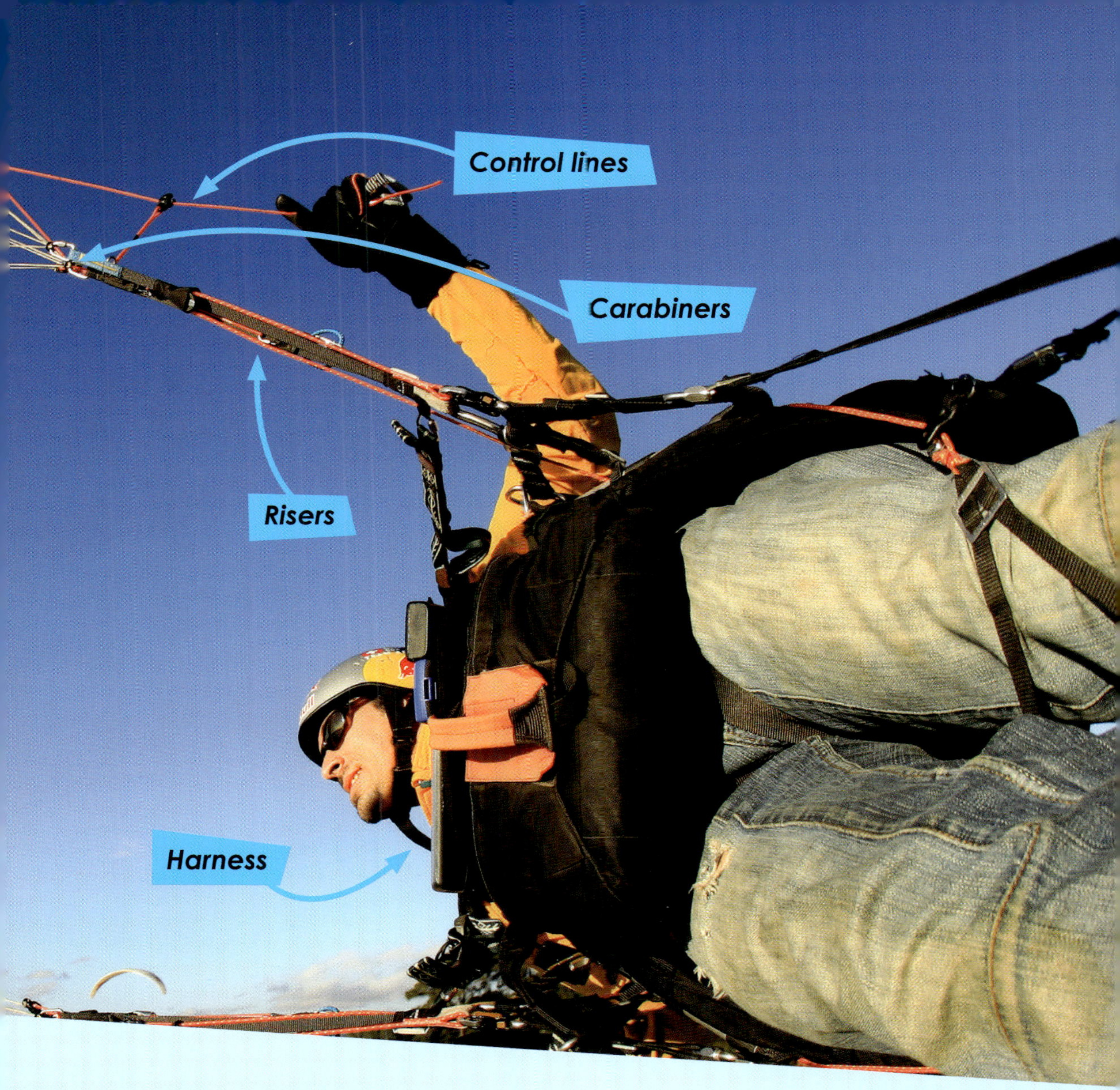

The lines come together close to the pilot and are joined to short strips of webbing called **risers.**

The risers are attached to the harness with small **carabiners.**

The **control lines** are usually called brakes. The brakes help the pilot to yaw the canopy.

LAUNCHING AND LANDING

Both types of glider are challenging to handle. Launching and landing can be especially difficult.

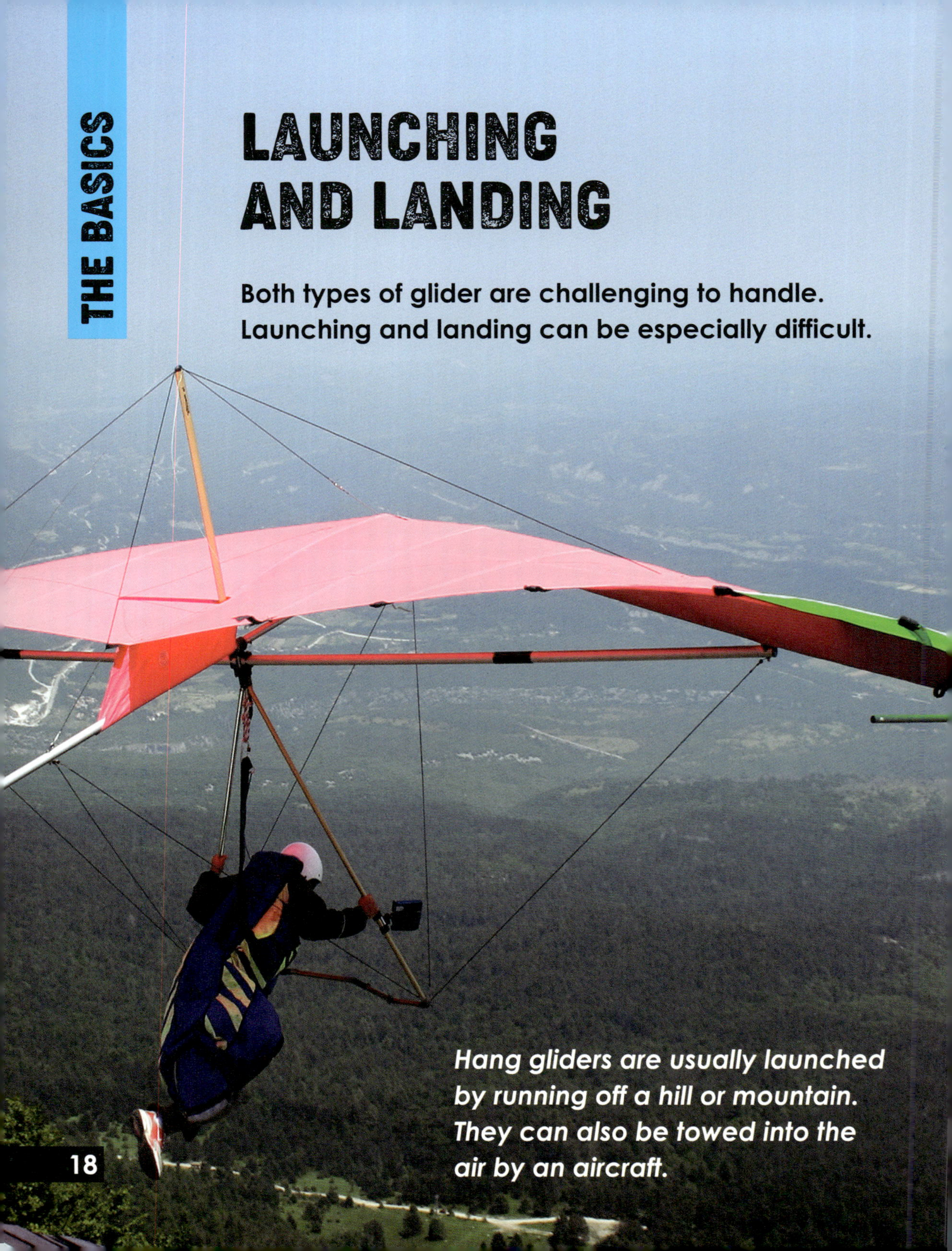

Hang gliders are usually launched by running off a hill or mountain. They can also be towed into the air by an aircraft.

Landing

To land a hang glider, the pilot first slows the wing. Next they hold the sides of the control frame to slow it down.

Launching

The trickiest part of paragliding is launching.

First, the wing is laid out on the ground. Then the lines are pulled to let in air. Finally, the risers are pulled to make the wing rise.

CLOTHING

Hang gliding pilots need to dress for cold conditions, even though it may be warm on the ground.

High climbers

The higher gliders go, the colder the air becomes. Gliders can reach over 15,000 feet (4,500 m). At this height, the average temperature is 1.4 °F (-17°C).

Helmet

A helmet is a must. Head injuries can be very serious. For high flights, a warm hat is worn under the helmet.

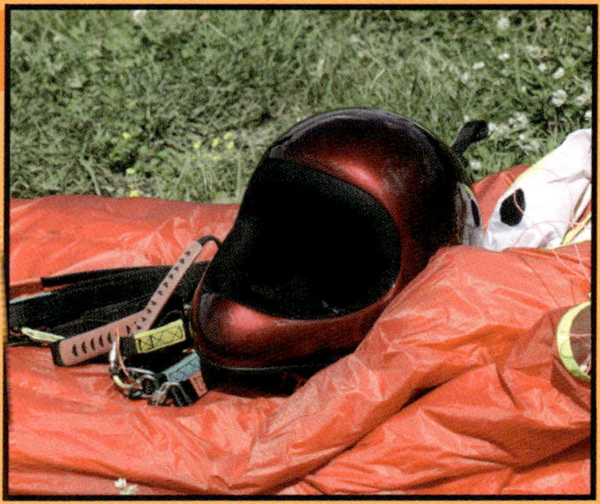

Goggles

Sunglasses or goggles are essential. Eye-damaging UV rays in sunlight are much stronger at high altitudes.

Flying suit

A one-piece flying suit is worn for paragliding.

Hang glider pilots fly in warm harnesses, so they usually just wear windproof jackets.

EXTRA PROTECTION

Pilots also need the following equipment for protection.

Speedy arms

To make themselves go faster, pilots wear tight Lycra sleeves over their flying clothes. This keeps down the drag from their bodies.

Warm hands and feet

Gloves or mittens need to be worn, whatever the weather. Without gloves, it is easy to hurt your hands on the control lines.

Good boots are needed to protect your feet.

Sun protection

Always use strong sunscreen as the sun can easily burn you.

EQUIPMENT

Pilots carry instruments so they don't get lost.

A hang glider pilot lies in the harness and has the instruments on the control frame.

Paragliders have the instruments in a waist pack that is clipped to the harness.

Pilots carry a special map that shows airports and routes, called airways.

It is important that glider pilots keep clear of airways that airplanes might be on.

Here is a list of the instruments used:

Altimeter Shows the glider's height.

Variometer ('vario') Shows how fast the glider is climbing or sinking. It is dangerous to rise too fast or high.

GPS Shows the glider's route.

Two-way radio Sends out emergency signals.

SAFETY

Gliding accidents can happen often. Most pilots carry a rescue parachute, which is only used in a real emergency.

The rescue chute is joined to the glider by a strong line called a strop.

Landing protection

Landings can go wrong, so harnesses have built-in safety features. One safety feature is a thick layer of foam to protect the pilot's spine.

The spine protection is built into the back

A knife with a protected blade to cut away the parachute if needed

Landings can cause serious injuries. When landing, pilots must keep their feet together and knees bent.

In wooded areas, pilots carry a long cord to help them climb down if they land in a tree!

Students on their early flights are kept close to the ground by instructors using ropes

TYPES OF GLIDER

Competition and training gliders are flown in the same way, but competition gliders can go much faster.

In competitions, the aim is to fly a route across country as quickly as possible. Pilots have to find lots of areas of rising air (lift).

A competition glider being tow-launched by a microlight tug

A fast glide is good when flying from one area of lift to another.

A very stiff wing is faster but is difficult to turn. Pilots use a cord to help them to turn.

The stiffer the wing, the faster the glider

A Swift'Light in flight

THE SWIFT

Developed in 1989, the Swift was a special type of hang glider. It had extremely stiff wings and flaps to help to steer it like a plane. It has been replaced with a newer version, the 'Swift'Light'.

Swift pilots sit in small cockpits with a door in the bottom. Swifts can be launched like other hang gliders. Once they are off the ground, the pilots pull their legs up, close the door and control the Swift with a joystick.

Swifts are not easy to carry. The wings cannot be rolled up. It takes two people to launch a Swift.

RIGIDS

The rigid came along in the early 1990s. It has a carbon fiber frame. The rigid is very light and strong, with a very stiff wing.

When the pilot swings sideways, he operates flaps called spoilers on top of the wings. When a spoiler lifts up, the glider turns to that side.

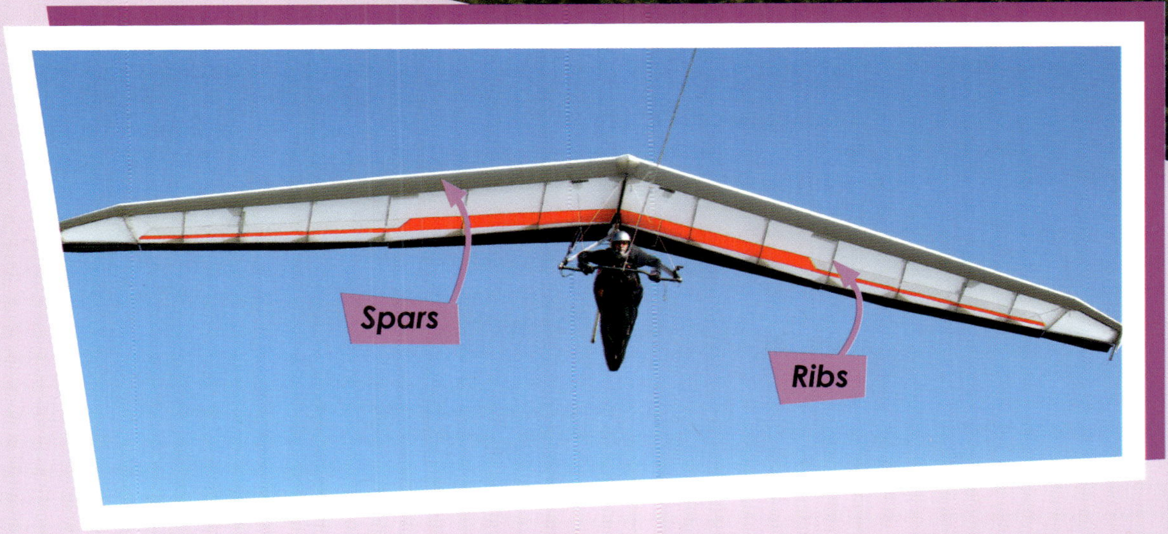

A rigid is strong because of its long carbon fiber spars and ribs.

TYPES OF PARAGLIDER

There are training paragliders and competition gliders. Training gliders are slow and stable. Competition gliders are fast, but hard to fly.

A training paraglider

A competition paraglider

Wing tips can sometimes collapse in turbulence, but can ususally be recovered easily

Competition gliders are flown only by experts at events like the World Championships.

Here are the main features of a competition glider:

- The canopy is wider and thinner.
- There are more cells in the canopy.
- The cells are smaller.
- The lines are much thinner. This helps with the wind.
- There is a foot-operated bar for more speed.
- The harness is slightly curved.

GLIDER CONTESTS

The starting age for hang gliding and paragliding competitions is sixteen.

There are several types of contests for gliders: cross-country racing, landing accuracy, aerobatics, speed flying and record breaking.

Hang gliders reach the inflatable finishing line after a speed race

Cross-country racing

The competitors record their flights on their GPS instruments. Every competitor's flight is downloaded from their GPS to work out how well they've done.

Landing accuracy competitions

For this competition, pilots have to make a stand-up landing on a target.

Hitting the spot is much harder than it looks, especially if the wind is strong.

AEROBATICS

Aerobatic (acro) flying on hang gliders or paragliders is a very special skill.

Acro competitions usually take place over a lake.

Pilots are scored for the difficulty of the things they do and on how good they look in the air.

An acro pilot preparing to land on a raft in a lake

Othar Lawrence performing a wing-over

Each trick has a special name. Some tricks involve loops and high-speed spirals.

The first Acro World Championships were near Montreux, Switzerland, in 2005.

SPEED FLYING

Speed flying takes place in the mountains. It is a mix of skiing and paragliding. This is a sport for experts only!

Speed fliers use small paragliders and wear skis. They skim down the mountainside, less than 3 feet (1 m) above the ground. Speed flying is thrilling but very dangerous.

Speed flying in the French Alps

Competition speed flying

Hang gliders sometimes fly in downhill races called speed gliding.

The pilot launches a glider from a ramp and races down the mountain. They must pass underneath and between gates.

Speed gliders travel up to 80 miles per hour (130 km/h)!

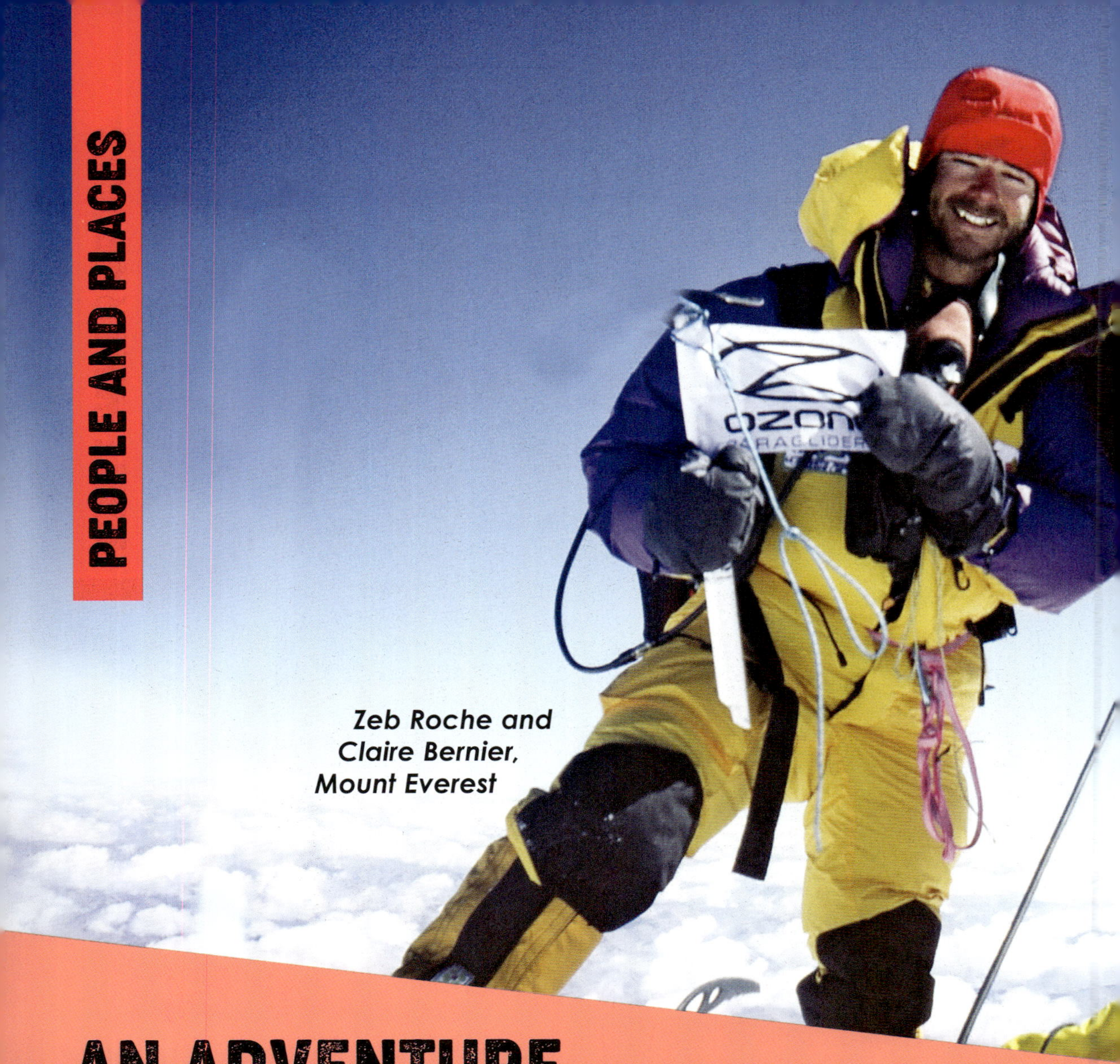

Zeb Roche and Claire Bernier, Mount Everest

AN ADVENTURE

French couple Zeb Roche and Claire Bernier set themselves an adventurous task. They decided to fly off the tops of the highest mountains in each of the seven continents of the world.

Tandem paraglider

Flying as a passenger in a two-seat paraglider (a tandem) can be a good way to experience gliding for the first time.

Zeb and Claire are talented paragliders. It took them almost six years to complete their task. They set off in 1996 using a two-seat paraglider.

PEOPLE AND PLACES

AMAZING STUNTS

Felix and Raul Rodriguez are stars of paragliding acro. They are world famous for their solo and pair performances.

Mike Küng

In 2004, Mike Küng launched from a hot-air balloon at 33,136 feet (10,100 m). He needed an oxygen mask, and was covered in 0.8 inches (2 cm) of ice!

Mike Küng launching himself out of a hot-air balloon

John Heiney performing a loop

John Heiney

American, John Heiney held the record for the most consecutive loops with a hang glider. Chad Elchin now holds the record with 95 loops (July 2001).

GLOSSARY

Acro Short for aerobatics; loops, spins, wing-overs and other aerial stunts performed with a paraglider.

Altimeter An instrument that shows the height of a glider.

Battens The stiffening ribs used for wings.

Brakes The control lines of a paraglider.

Cells The individual divisions that make up a paraglider wing.

Control frame The triangular frame that the pilot uses to control the glider.

Gliding The sport of unpowered flying that uses thermals and other forms of natural lift.

GPS Global Positioning System.

Joystick An aircraft control lever used on the Swift.

Keel The tube running down the middle of the hang glider.

Leading edge The front edge of a glider wing.

Lift Rising air. Also used to describe the power generated by a wing moving through the air.

Microlight tug A small light aircraft with up to two seats that is used to launch gliders by towing them into the air.

Ram-air effect The way in which a paraglider wing keeps its shape.

Risers The straps between a paraglider's lines and the harness.

Rogallo An early hang glider named after Dr Francis Rogallo.

Spoilers The flaps on top of a wing that stop the lift, making a glider turn.

Thermals The upward currents of warm air that are used by birds and gliders to gain height.

Trailing edge The rear edge of a glider wing.

Variometer An instrument that shows whether a glider is climbing or sinking. It is essential for all gliders, because it is impossible to tell whether you are going up or down once you are hundreds of feet above the ground.

INDEX